KT-431-369

C334597350

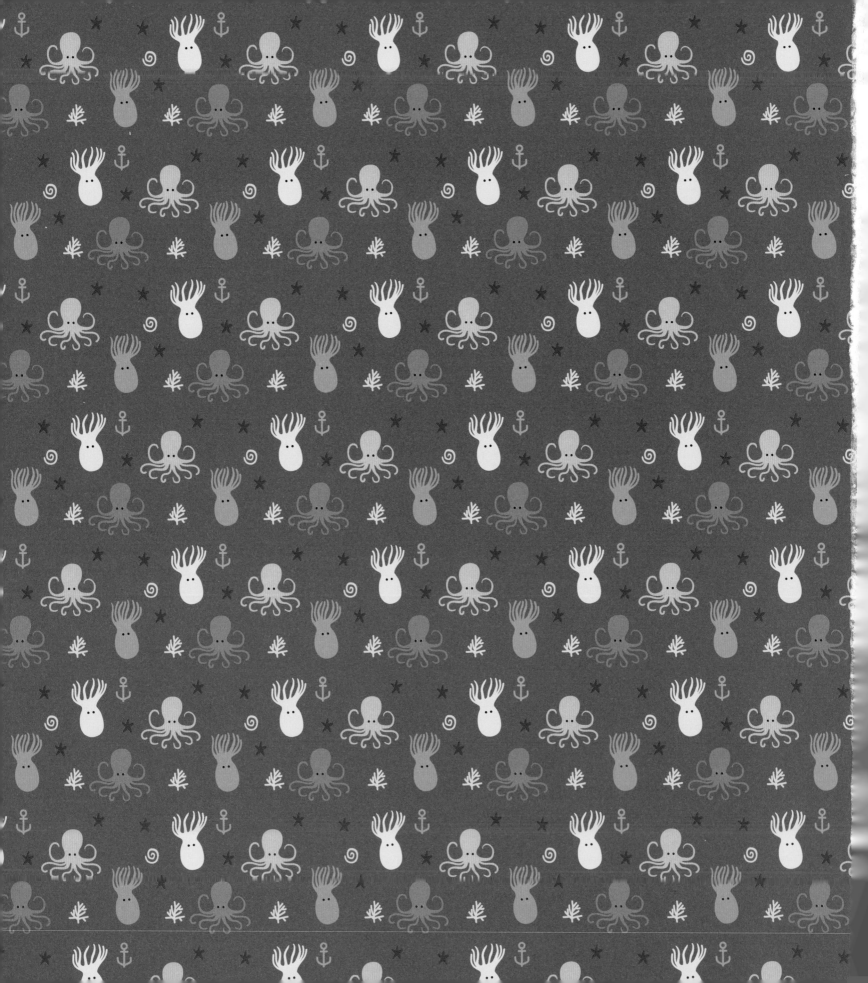

This octopus belongs to:

....

Dedicated to the Sea Change Project and brilliant little octopuses everywhere – G. D.

For the Allish twins, Charles and Sophia – A. B.

First published in the United Kingdom in 2021 by Thames & Hudson Ltd, 181A High Holborn, London WC1V 7QX

If I had an octopus © 2021 Thames & Hudson Ltd, London
Text © 2020 Gabby Dawnay
Illustrations © 2021 Alex Barrow

All Rights Reserved. No part of this publication may be reproduced or transmitted in any form or by any means, electronic or mechanical, including photocopy, recording or any other information storage and retrieval system, without prior permission in writing from the publisher.

British Library Cataloguing-in-Publication Data
A catalogue record for this book is available from the British Library

ISBN 978-0-500-65225-1

Printed and bound in China by Everbest Printing Co. Ltd

Be the first to know about our new releases, exclusive content and author events by visiting
thamesandhudson.com
thamesandhudsonusa.com
thamesandhudson.com.au

GABBY DAWNAY
ALEX BARROW

If I had an
OCTOPUS

I do like 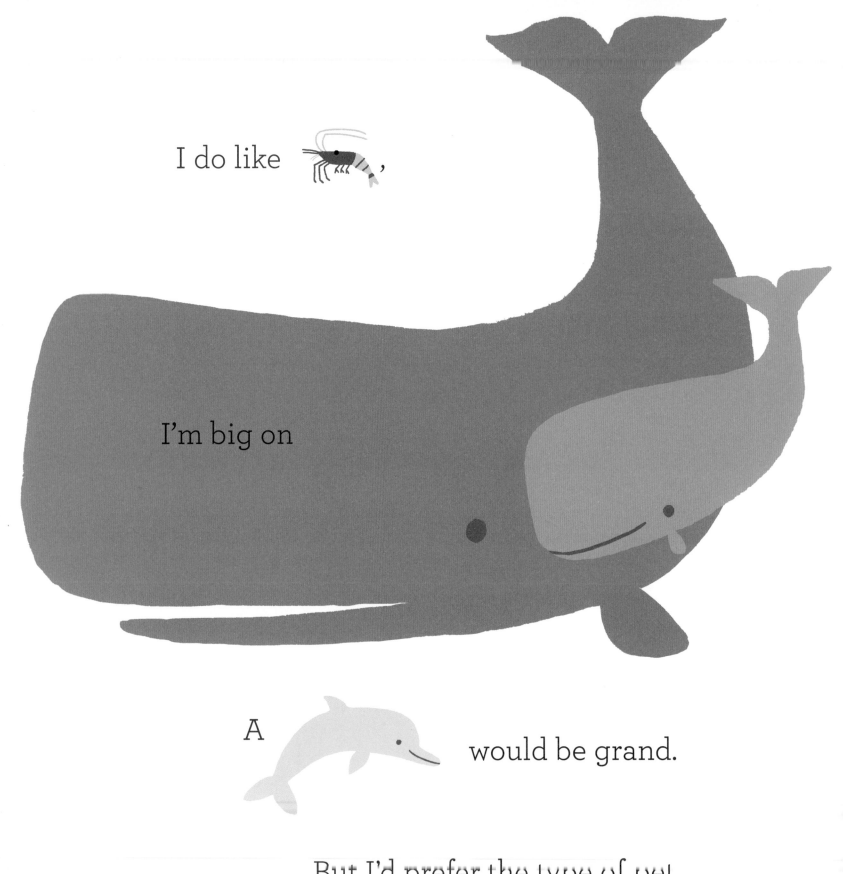,

I'm big on

A   would be grand.

But I'd prefer the type of pet
that wants to hold my hand.

A  ? Too wobbly!

A  ? Too many claws!

A  perhaps?

Though sharks have tons
of teeth inside their...

J A W S!

I really want a CLEVER pet,
a pet with many charms...
The sort of pet with talents
and a large amount of arms.

Oh, if I had an **OCTOPUS**...

we'd 'ripple' down the street,
my octopus on tentacles
and me upon my feet.

All my friends would like to play,
they'd only have to ask
for football, tennis, anything –
my pet could multi-task!

My octopus would teach me
how to add and calculate.

We'd practise on her tentacles
by counting up to eight!

If I had an octopus
she'd help me with my sums
so we could play all afternoon

– my octopus on drums!

Each day my octopus would cook
a very special dish...

I'd help her stir a stew of prawns
and other kinds of fish!

Octopuses have no bones
so fit in any place.
They squeeze through even tiny
gaps and never leave a trace...

My octopus would be the best at painting, don't you think?

But careful not to shock her or she'll cover you in...

....!

As well as being inky
and extremely good at art,
my octopus would tidy up
to keep things looking smart!

Imagine what a thrill it is
to blend into a wall
and be so good at camouflage
you can't be seen at all!

An octopus has eight long arms
to hug me nice and tight.

They also have three beating hearts
to love with all their might.

My octopus would juggle books
and read them one by one –
a bedtime filled with stories
sounds like extra-special fun!

Then finally we'd fall asleep,
my octopus and me,
and dream of our adventures
at the bottom of the sea...

If you'd rather have a giant pet,
you might like to read
If I had a dinosaur.

Or for a more relaxing story,
try *If I had a sleepy sloth.*

But if you feel like a truly
magical tale, pick up
If I had a unicorn.

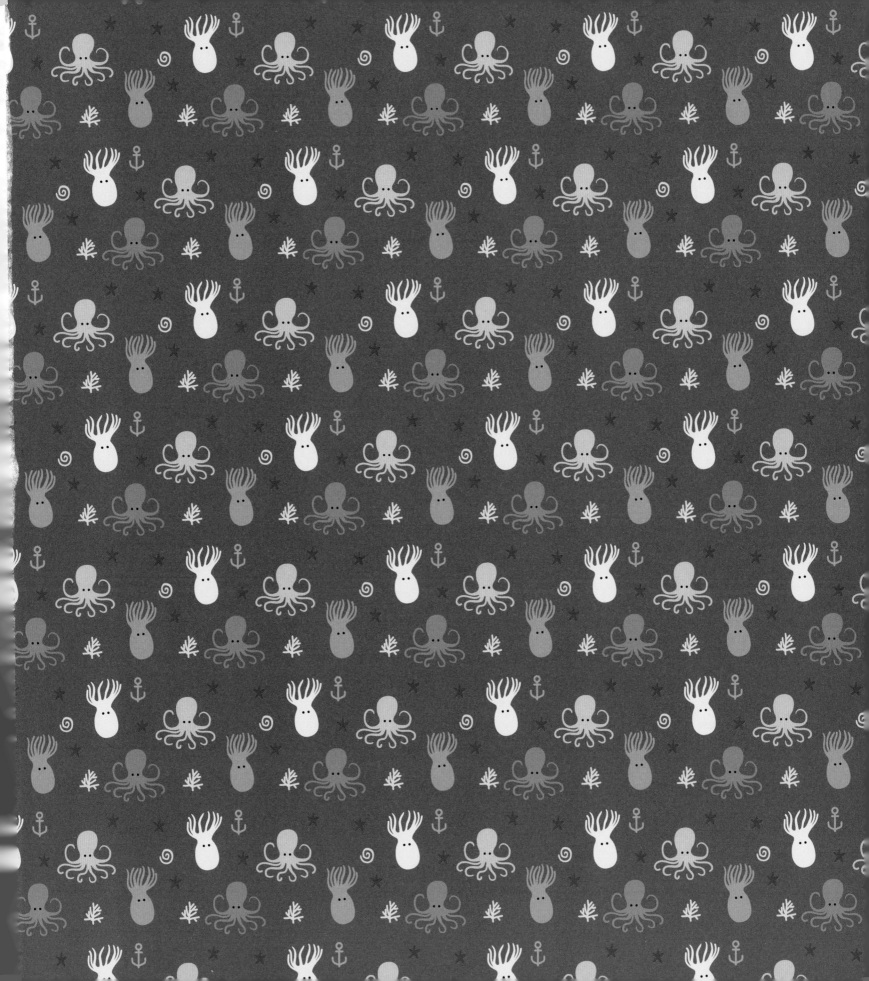

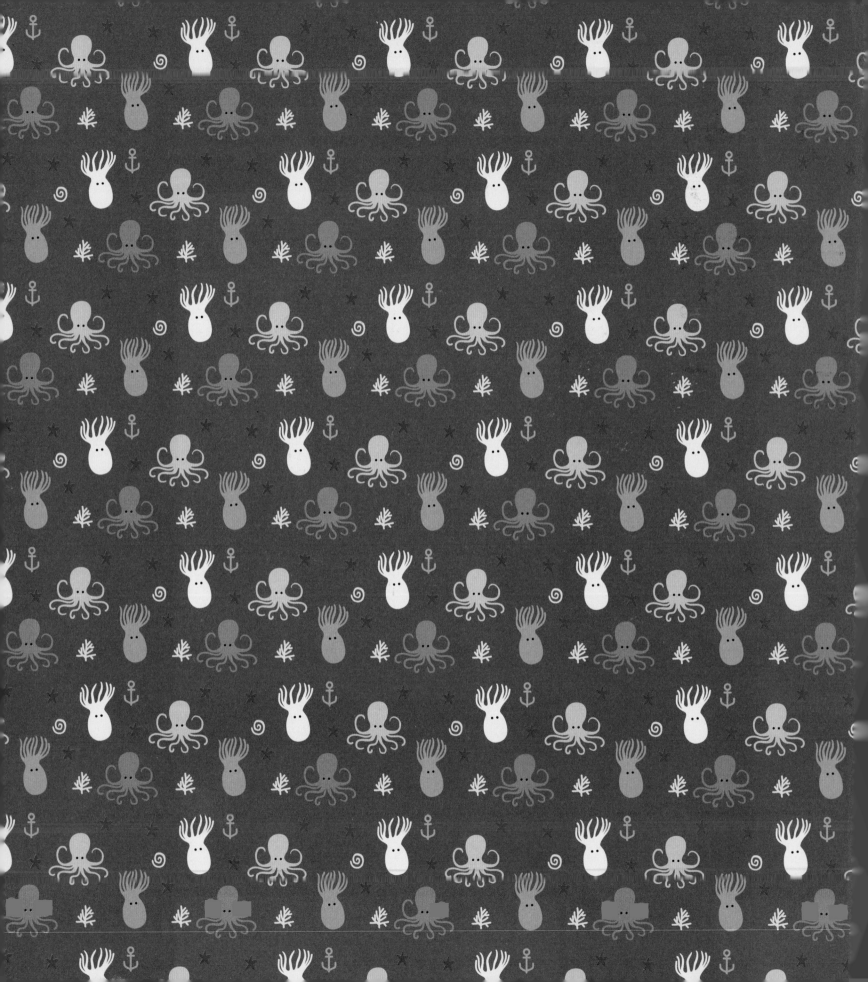

KT-198-339

9030 00007 7008 5

CHRISTMAS

by Emily Raij

raintree
a Capstone company — publishers for children

Raintree is an imprint of Capstone Global Library Limited, a company incorporated in England and Wales having its registered office at 264 Banbury Road, Oxford, OX2 7DY – Registered company number: 6695582

www.raintree.co.uk
myorders@raintree.co.uk

Text © Capstone Global Library Limited 2022
The moral rights of the proprietor have been asserted.

All rights reserved. No part of this publication may be reproduced in any form or by any means (including photocopying or storing it in any medium by electronic means and whether or not transiently or incidentally to some other use of this publication) without the written permission of the copyright owner, except in accordance with the provisions of the Copyright, Designs and Patents Act 1988 or under the terms of a licence issued by the Copyright Licensing Agency, 5th Floor, Shackleton House, 4 Battle Bridge Lane, London SE1 2HX (www.cla.co.uk). Applications for the copyright owner's written permission should be addressed to the publisher.

Edited by Erika L Shores
Designed by Dina Her
Original illustrations © Capstone Global Library Limited 2022
Picture research by Jo Miller
Production by Tori Abraham
Originated by Capstone Global Library Ltd
Printed and bound in India

978 1 3982 1297 8 (hardback)
978 1 3982 1361 6 (paperback)

British Library Cataloguing in Publication Data
A full catalogue record for this book is available from the British Library.

Acknowledgements
We would like to thank the following for permission to reproduce photographs: Alamy: Chad Ehlers, 17; Getty Images: aldomurillo, 18, Craig Lovell, 19, GraphicaArtis/Contributor, 26, lisegagne, 21; Newscom: Polaris/Damien Alitti, 14, ZUMA Press/Arroyo Fernandez, 22; Shutterstock: anon_tae, 11, CKP1001, 27, DGLimages, 5, EQRoy, 15, Firn, 12, Hans Christiansson, 16, Jan S., 13, Kit Leong, 8, MestoSveta, 1, Monkey Business Images, 29, Nowaczyk, 9, Rawpixel.com, 25, Sandra Cunningham, Cover, Zvonimir Atletic, 7. Artistic elements: Shutterstock: Rafal Kulik.

Every effort has been made to contact copyright holders of material reproduced in this book. Any omissions will be rectified in subsequent printings if notice is given to the publisher.

All the internet addresses (URLs) given in this boo[k]
press. However, due to the dynamic nature of the i[nternet, some addresses may have]
changed, or sites may have changed or ceased to [exist since publication. While the]
author and publisher regret any inconvenience thi[s may cause readers, no responsibility]
for any such changes can be accepted by either th[e author or the publisher.]

LONDON BOROUGH OF WANDSWORTH	
9030 00007 7008 5	
Askews & Holts	P vtC
J394.266 JUNIOR NON-	1/22
RAN J	WW21011871

CONTENTS

Words in **bold** are in the glossary.

WHAT IS CHRISTMAS?

Lights glow on houses and trees. People sing songs in churches. Families are at home together. It is Christmas.

Christmas is a holiday. Christians around the world celebrate it. Christianity is a religion that follows the teachings of Jesus. The Bible says Jesus is the son of God. Christmas celebrates the birth of Jesus.

People share the story of Jesus's birth at Christmas. His parents were Mary and Joseph. They walked a long way to the town of Bethlehem. When they arrived, there was nowhere for them to stay. Mary was about to give birth.

Mary and Joseph found a barn with animals. Jesus was born there. They put baby Jesus in a manger. That is a box full of hay for animals to eat.

The Bible says when Jesus was born, three kings saw a star shine in the sky. They thought it meant the son of God had been born. The kings followed the star to Bethlehem. They found Jesus. They gave him gifts.

WHEN IS CHRISTMAS?

Many countries celebrate Christmas on 25 December. Others celebrate in January. They use a different calendar. It shows that Jesus was born later. The night before Christmas is Christmas Eve. Christians often go to church very late that night. Some go the next morning, on Christmas Day.

A Christmas tree in Peru in South America

In the northern part of the world, Christmas is in winter. In the southern part, Christmas is in summer. Seasons are opposite in these two parts of the world.

WHO CELEBRATES CHRISTMAS?

Christians in many countries celebrate Christmas. They honour the birth of Jesus. In the early 1900s, many non-Christians began celebrating Christmas too. They liked the traditions and time spent together.

Today, people enjoy many Christmas **customs**. Most eat meals with loved ones and give gifts. Some people decorate trees and their homes. Many adults make Christmas special for children. People young and old enjoy being with each other for this holiday.

HOW DO PEOPLE CELEBRATE CHRISTMAS AROUND THE WORLD?

Many Christmas traditions started in Germany. Baking cookies is one. Germans also decorate trees on Christmas Eve. On Christmas Day, many people go to church. They continue the celebration on 26 December with loved ones. The season ends on 6 January. This is called Three Kings Day.

German Christmas cookies

Christmas markets are popular in Germany. People buy food, toys and decorations. They watch plays. They listen to music.

A Christmas market in Dresden, Germany

In France, the feast of Saint Nicholas starts the season on 6 December. Children get treats to celebrate the kind Saint Nicholas. He helped poor children. People set up dolls to show Jesus's birth. Many attend Christmas plays. People also decorate trees.

Children visit Saint Nicholas in France.

A kings' cake

French people go to church late on Christmas Eve. Then they have a special meal. Children leave their shoes by the fireplace. They hope Father Christmas will fill them with treats. **Epiphany** ends the season on 6 January. People eat a special kings' cake.

Advent is the four weeks leading up to Christmas. This is a special time in Sweden. Saint Lucia Day is on 13 December. The oldest girl in the family dresses up as Saint Lucia. She wears a white robe and a crown of candles.

People hang Advent stars in their windows. They light Advent candles. They decorate trees with flags and ornaments. People share a big meal. It is called a smorgasbord.

Sweden's Christmas season ends on 13 January. That is Saint Knut's Day. People take down trees. They eat homemade sweets that had been placed on the tree.

A smorgasbord

Las Posadas is a Mexican tradition. This celebration starts on 16 December. It lasts until 24 December. Children go door to door asking for a place to sleep, the way Mary and Joseph did. Children hand out Mary and Joseph dolls.

Each day ends with a meal. Then children hit open **piñatas**. Bells ring. Fireworks fill the sky. Red poinsettia flowers decorate homes and streets.

Children lead a parade to church on Christmas Eve. They place a baby Jesus doll there. People also go to church on Christmas Day. Mexico's Christmas season ends on 2 February with Candlemas. Candles are blessed for the new year.

In countries such as the UK, Canada and Australia, 26 December is also a holiday. It is called Boxing Day.

Long ago, people would put gifts in a box to thank workers after Christmas. That's how the holiday got its name.

Today on Boxing Day, some people still give to people in need. Others go shopping, watch films or go to sporting events.

On Boxing Day, people skate on an outdoor rink in Amsterdam, the Netherlands.

On Boxing Day, people skate on an outdoor rink in Amsterdam, the Netherlands.

Some countries celebrate Boxing Day as a second Christmas Day. Poland, Hungary, Germany, Romania and the Netherlands do this. The countries of Bulgaria, Czechia and Slovakia also have Boxing Day.

Some countries celebrate Christmas 13 to 14 days after 25 December. Russia, Ukraine, Ethiopia and some other countries use a different church calendar. That calendar has the birth of Jesus on a later date.

HOW DO WE CELEBRATE CHRISTMAS?

Many people enjoy spending time with family and friends at Christmas. Often, families have their own special traditions for the food they eat and the decorations they put up.

Some Christmas traditions come from other countries. These customs include decorating **artificial** or fresh evergreen trees with lights and **ornaments**. Stars or angels are put on top. People put presents under the tree to open on Christmas morning.

Father Christmas is a part of some people's traditions. He is said to live at the North Pole. On Christmas Eve, Father Christmas rides on a sleigh. It is pulled by reindeer. He brings gifts to children. Father Christmas is a symbol of the giving spirit of Christmas.

Some people hang Christmas stockings at home. Small presents are placed inside.

People enjoy many Christmas stories and favourite films each year. Some people like to sing Christmas songs. These are called carols. People sing in church and schools. Some people go from door to door singing carols and collecting money for charity.

Some people put up Christmas lights on their homes or in their gardens. They show their trees in their front windows.

Around the world, Christmas and its traditions are important to many people.

GLOSSARY

Advent special time to prepare for Christmas

artificial not real

carol joyful song sung at Christmas

celebrate do something fun on a special day

custom tradition in a culture or society

Epiphany Christian festival held on 6 January in honour of the coming of the three kings to the infant Jesus Christ

feast large, fancy meal for a lot of people on a special occasion

ornament decoration hung on a Christmas tree

piñata hollow, decorated container filled with sweets or toys; a person tries to break the piñata with a stick

posada special Mexican Christmas celebration

FIND OUT MORE

BOOKS

Celebrating Christian Festivals (Celebration Days), Nick Hunter (Raintree, 2016)

Celebrations Around the World: The Fabulous Celebrations You Won't Want to Miss, Katy Halford (DK Children, 2019)

Children Just Like Me: A New Celebration of Children Around the World, DK (DK Children, 2016)

WEBSITES

www.bbc.co.uk/bitesize/topics/z478gwx/articles/zb33pg8
Learn more about different celebrations.

www.dkfindout.com/uk/more-find-out/festivals-and-holidays
Find out more about festivals and holidays around the world.

INDEX